Becky 1986
Happy 7th Birthday
From Andrea

Published 1984 by
The Hamlyn Publishing Group Limited
London · New York · Sydney · Toronto
Astronaut House, Feltham, Middlesex, England
© Mansell Print Limited 1984

ISBN 0 600 38944 8

Printed in Italy

Bubbles and Troubles

By Simon Joyner

Hamlyn

London · New York · Sydney · Toronto

It was a bright Autumn morning in Misty Wood. Gordon and Gloria Grub were enjoying a nice crunchy acorn breakfast.

'Look, Gordon, you can tell it's Autumn,' said Gloria. 'There are only four leaves left on this oak tree.'

'Only three now,' said Gordon, as one more leaf floated to the ground.

'Oh, look Gordon!' cried Gloria suddenly.
'Here comes the Autumn mist.'

'You can see now how Misty Wood got its
name,' Gordon coughed.

The mist got so thick that Gordon and
Gloria could hardly see each other.

What Gordon and Gloria didn't realise was that the mist wasn't really a mist at all. It was clouds of dust made by Minnie Shrew. She was busy sweeping up leaves and brushing out the trees.

Minnie was getting ready for the Nut and Berry Harvest: the day when all the animals in Misty Wood collected enough food to see them through the long cold months of Winter.

Gilbert Mouse was busy looking for fallen crab-apples. He was going to make crab-apple wine. Suddenly he saw lots of prickles in the undergrowth.

'That's a funny-looking berry,' he thought and then realised it was Henry Hedgehog. 'Hello, Henry, what are you doing?' he asked.

'You've heard of the dandelion clock,' said
Henry. 'Well, I've just invented a dandelion
watch.'

'Does it work?' Gilbert asked.
'Of course,' said Henry.
'All right then,' Gilbert chuckled. 'What's the time?'
Henry took a deep breath and blew . . .

'One o'clock,' Henry said proudly.
'Thank you,' said Gilbert, rather crossly.

Henry was very fond of Gilbert's crab-apple wine, so he decided to go off and look for crab-apples too. He hadn't gone very far when he came across a huge crab-apple lying by some toadstools in a clump of dead leaves.

'What a beauty!' Henry cried, picking it up. 'It looks so good I won't give it to Gilbert. I'll eat it for my lunch instead.'

But just as he was about to take a large bite, a little voice beside him whispered, 'Excuse me, Henry. Would you mind if I and a few friends took a tiny bit of your apple?'

'Of course not,' Henry replied. 'It's so large that there's plenty for all of us.'

'Oh, thank you, Henry,' said Graham Grub. He turned round and shouted: 'Lunchtime, everyone!'

Suddenly, Henry was surrounded by hungry grubs.

When things had died down, Graham gave
Henry what was left of his lunch.

Henry was not at all amused. 'Now look
here, you greedy grubs,' he started to say.
But he found he was only talking to the
apple core. All the grubs had run away to
look for blackberries.

After a long search, the grubs came across the fattest, juiciest blackberries they'd ever seen. How their mouths watered.

'There's just one snag,' said Gloria. 'When we've picked them, how are we going to get them all home?'

'I know,' said Graham. 'We'll make grass baskets.'

So they all set about making baskets out of blades of grass. Haven't they made a neat job?

When they had finished, Gloria suggested that Graham should stay behind to look after the baskets. For Graham was very greedy, and Gloria knew that if he was let loose in the blackberry bush, there would be very few left to collect.

'Oh, all right,' said Graham crossly.

But when the grubs returned with armfuls
of blackberries, they found that greedy
Graham had eaten all the grass baskets, and
was just finishing off the last handle!

'Oh, really Graham,' said Gloria crossly.
'Now how do you think we're going to carry
the blackberries home?'

Just at that moment, Sidney Snail came
crawling up.

Sidney and the grubs thought hard about the problem.

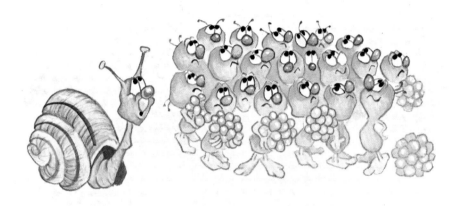

Then, suddenly, all the grubs had the same idea at the same time.

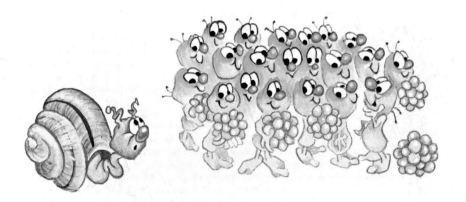

'Your shell makes a perfect blackberry
holder, Sidney,' said Gloria, and promised to
bring it back soon.

Meanwhile, Gilbert was in his kitchen busily stirring a large tub full of crab-apples.
'This is going to be the best brew I've ever made,' he told his helpers.

After consulting his great-great-great grandfather's recipe book, Gilbert added the secret ingredients – essence of toadflax, truffle juice and pigswort pollen.

'This will taste delicious,' smiled Gilbert.

Now came the part Gilbert always enjoyed most. Filling a large ladle, he took a great big gulp.

'What's the matter, Gilbert?' asked one of the grubs.

'I forgot to add any sugar,' he mumbled, turning a very funny colour.

After adding a whole bag of sugar and giving the brew a good stir, Gilbert decided to have another taste. This time, however, he was very careful to try just one single drop.

But it was far too fizzy! The grubs watched
in amazement as Gilbert exploded around the
kitchen.

'Never mind about Pop goes the Weasel,
it's Pop goes Gilbert Mouse,' they laughed.

Just then there was a knock on the door and Henry walked in.

'You look as though you've drunk too much wine already,' said Henry. 'How's it coming along?'

'I'm still working on it,' said Gilbert wearily.

'Well, I've got a few friends outside who are waiting to give you a surprise! This will really cheer you up,' Henry said. 'Come on in everyone!'

All Gilbert's friends came into the kitchen.

'I'm sorry, everyone,' Gilbert said. 'The wine isn't – er – quite ready yet.'

'Never mind,' said Minnie Shrew, 'we can eat this instead,' and she presented him with a magnificent cheesecake.